A BUTTON
IN HER EAR

Concept Book

A Button in Her Ear

By *Ada B. Litchfield*

Pictures by *Eleanor Mill*

ALBERT WHITMAN & *Company, Morton Grove, Illinois*

This book is dedicated to Althea M. Ross,
who already knows why. . .—A.B.L.

The author wishes to express appreciation to Sister Anne Conway, CSJ, Supervisor of the Middle School of The Boston School for the Deaf for many helpful suggestions. Appreciation is also expressed to Sister Declan Sullivan, CSJ, and Sister Margaret McDonald, CSJ, of the Audiology Department for demonstrating a hearing test and the use and care of a hearing aid.

Library of Congress Cataloging-in-Publication Data
Litchfield, Ada Bassett.
 A button in her ear.

 SUMMARY: A little girl relates how her hearing deficiency is detected and corrected with the use of a hearing aid.
  1. Hearing aids—Juvenile literature.
  2. Hearing disorders—Juvenile literature.
  [1. Hearing aids.   2.   Hearing disorders]
  I.   Mill, Eleanor.   II. Title.
  RF300.L57   617.8'9   75-28390
  ISBN 0-8075-0987-6

A Note About Angela's Story

A surprisingly large number of schoolchildren, about seven percent, have some degree of hearing loss. Where this loss is severe, it may be identified early; but where there is less serious impairment, discovery may come later and even accidentally.

In this story, Angela's hearing loss is suspected by her parents when her response to spoken words makes no sense. This is especially the case when Angela is unable to see the speaker and has no facial clues or lip movements to help her guess what is being said.

Because hearing loss may be due to illness or accident, or may be present from birth, Angela's parents take her to her own doctor, or pediatrician. He, in turn, after examination refers Angela to an audiologist, or hearing specialist. Using appropriate equipment, the audiologist determines the degree of hearing loss and its character. While one visit to this specialist is described in the story, Angela may indeed over a period of time make a series of visits to the audiologist for tests, consultation, and help in using her hearing aid.

A hearing aid is of use with some types of hearing loss, but not all. Even with her aid, Angela will probably not hear exactly what other children hear. She may, for example, be unable to distinguish certain pitches. Angela may need some auditory training; children with more severe hearing loss may need training in using visual clues and in their own speech production. If loss is profound, other means of communication using visual clues, sign language, and finger spelling may be employed.

Her parents and teachers reenforce Angela's healthy attitude toward using a hearing aid. For children in similar circumstances this story has special meaning, but for other girls and boys, it sets the stage for new understandings.

My name is Angela Perkins,
and I haven't always had a button in my ear.

Maybe nobody would have discovered that I needed this button if my friend Buzzie hadn't started to mutter, mutter all the time.

One day he shouted, "Throw me the ball! Throw me the ball!" And I did.

What he really said was
"Throw it to Paul!"
And because I didn't, we
lost the game.

Buzzie was mad at me. But I was even madder at him. I was so mad at him that I threw his bat into the bushes.

Poor Buzzie. He was sort of upset, I guess. But I didn't care. He is a fresh kid.

Do you know what he yelled at me? He yelled, "Just wait. I'll give you a kiss."

A kiss! Aack.

Later I found out what he said was, "Just wait. I'll get you for this."

That did make more sense.

Buzzie just muttered, muttered, muttered. Every time he was It when we played touch-your-toes, touch-your-nose at school, he got me out.

Once when I was It I did some muttering myself and got him out.

"Now see how you like it," I said to him.

But it didn't make any difference to Buzzie. Mutter, mutter, mutter, just the same.

One day my teacher Miss Hicks looked out the window and said, "Tomorrow we're going to burn our sweaters."

My mother really got excited when I told her. Poor Miss Hicks — I'm glad my mother didn't call her.

I guess what Miss Hicks really said was, "Tomorrow we're going to learn our letters."

Because that's what we did.

I like to draw pictures. I drew a big fire engine for my little brother.

My father, who was reading the paper, said, "Why don't you take it to bed?"

I did, and my mother was terribly upset. She knew my father had said, "Why don't you make it red?"

Anyhow, my mother and my father talked it over. They took me to see a doctor.

Dr. Adams smiled at me and said, "You haven't got cotton in your ears, have you, Angela?"

"Of course not," I said. What a silly question!

"Well," he said, "maybe it's earwax." Then he took a silver gizmo with a light on it from a black box and looked into my ears.

"Nope," he said. "No cotton, no earwax, no beans, no marbles..."

I laughed. I wouldn't do a dumb thing like that.

"No fooling," he said to my parents. "Sometimes kids do poke things like beans or marbles into their ears. A bean or a marble can get lost in the ear canal and cause all kinds of trouble. But I don't see anything like that in Angela's ears."

Dr. Adams asked my mother questions about me and if I'd ever been very sick. He looked in my ears again and did some other things. Then he wrote something on a paper and gave it to my mother.

"Make her a new gown," he muttered.

My parents understood.

What he had really said was "Take her to Sue Brown." She was another doctor.

After Dr. Brown had said hello to me, she put me in a little room with one glass wall. She put headphones over my ears. I had to raise my hand every time I heard a beeping sound.

Dr. Brown went into another room and turned some dials. I could see her and my mother through the window.

I raised my hand whenever I heard a beep. Each time, Dr. Brown nodded and drew lines on a chart.

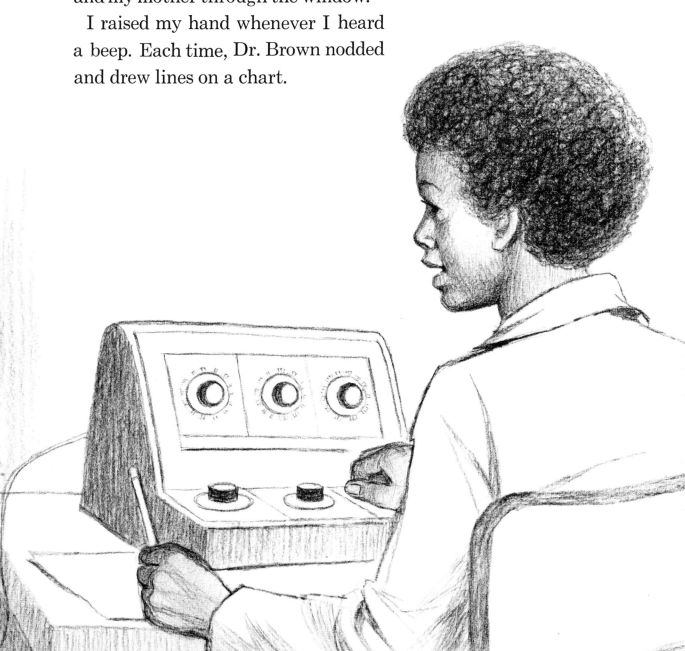

After awhile I took off the earphones and came out of the little room. I sat down on a stool beside my mother. Dr. Brown gave her the chart and said, "I think Angela needs a hearing aid."

"A hearing aid!" I screamed. "What's that?"

Dr. Brown took a hearing aid out of a drawer. She opened the box part and put in two tiny batteries. Then she held the earpiece close to my ear. I could hear her clearly when she said, "You can pretend this is a magic button, Angela. With it in your ear, you can usually hear what people say even when you can't see their lips move."

"So, OK," I said. "I guess that will be all right."

To myself I thought, "If it isn't, I'll get rid of it."

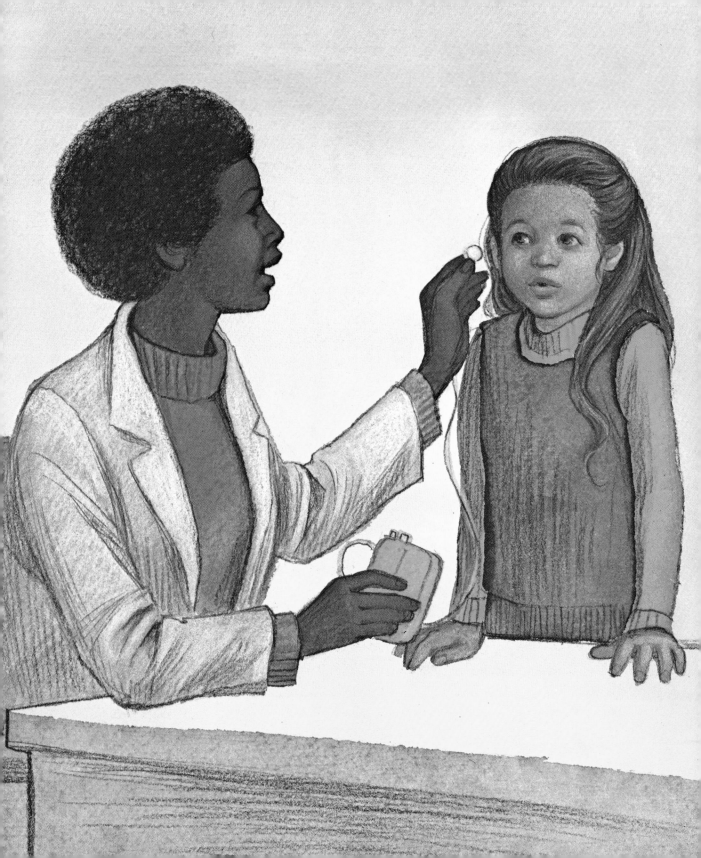

The man at the hearing aid center where I went to get my hearing aid was nice to me, too.

He showed me how to fit the button in my ear so that there wasn't any squealing noise. He showed me how to change the batteries. And he told my mother to buy a harness for me to wear that would hold the box part. Mother could make some extra ones, he said.

"Do I have to wear it all the time?" I asked. I was worried about that.

"No," he said. "You won't need your hearing aid when you're sleeping or playing rough games outdoors. You can wear it to school, when you go to the movies or watch TV. It will help you hear some of the things you're missing now."

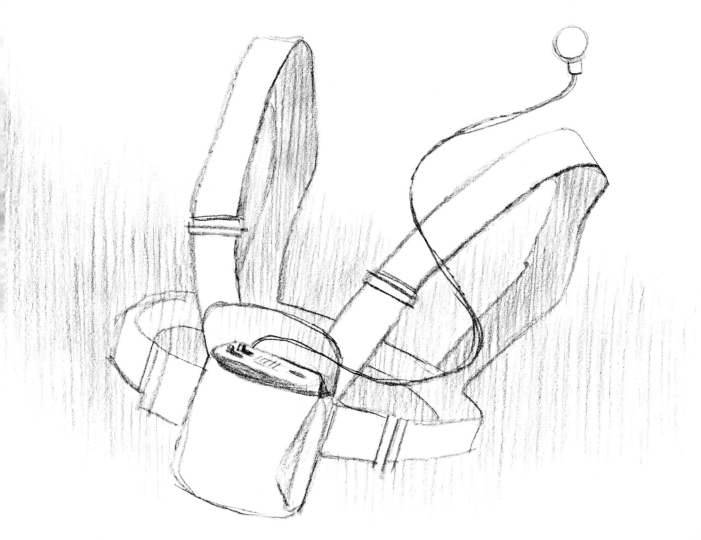

The next day I wore my hearing aid to school.
I wondered if anyone would notice it.

Miss Hicks has sharp eyes, I guess. She noticed
my hearing aid right away.

She asked very quietly if I would tell the kids
about it. I said I would.

Then Miss Hicks told everyone, "Angela is wearing something new today." She made it sound like a new locket or something for show-and-tell.

Everybody looked at me, and Miss Hicks said, "Just as Ann and Doug and John and I are wearing glasses to help us see better, so Angela is wearing a hearing aid to help her hear better."

Then she asked me to take the button out of my ear and my hearing aid out of its harness. I held them up so that everyone could see. I turned the button up, too high at first, and it squealed a little. Then I turned it down and let some of the kids hold the earpiece close to their ears.

They could hear what I hear when my hearing aid is working just right.

I opened the case to show the batteries and explained that I have to change them when the batteries go dead.

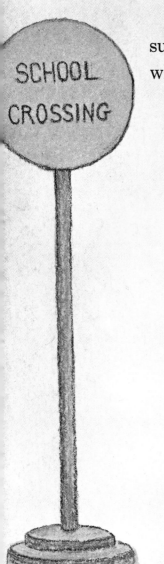

"Isn't that neat?" Miss Hicks said. And all the kids agreed. I think some of them even wished a little they could try a hearing aid, too.

Anyhow, here I am with a button in my ear. And in a way it is just like a magic button. I hear nearly everything anyone says to me.

I don't think someone is telling me to wade when I'm supposed to wait. And I hear everything Buzzie says when I listen.

But here's the special part. If I don't want to hear Buzzie talking, talking, and telling me how smart he is, here's what I do. I press this little gizmo and turn off my magic button.

Buzzie fades right out — just like that!

That makes Buzzie hopping-up-and-down-mad. And me winning-grinning glad.

So — a button in your ear is a good thing, if you need it.